THE NIGHT HAS TEETH

A Short Story

RANDY SPEEG

SASGORA BOOKS

The Night Has Teeth

THE NIGHT HAS TEETH

"Are you sure you don't want to pull over?" Carrie asked.

"Yes, I'm sure," Steve glared at her with a look that said *stop-nagging-me*.

"The rain is getting heavy," she said looking out through the windshield. The wipers squealed across the cold, foggy glass. Carrie leaned forward and switched on the defroster. "I can't even see the road signs anymore until we are right on top of them."

Steve heard the concern in her voice and the *good husband* side of his brain kicked in. "We're fine honey, it won't be that much longer before we get to the Virginia border. We'll out drive the rain before we get there," as the words came out, he wasn't even able to convince himself. Despite the many times he had driven across this semi-mountainous West Virginian highway, on their way to visit Carrie's folks, he still got disoriented. "Baby, can you turn on the radio, maybe we can find a weather report?"

The report given by the radio's static ridden voice did nothing to sooth Carrie's nerves. The rain would continue throughout the night. She looked out her window at the trees, shadowy hulks climbing up into the gloomy night. The forest beside them brightened with a flash of lightning.

"What was that?" Carrie gasped.

"What was what?"

"I saw something, out there."

"I was watching the road hun, was it an animal... road kill?"

Thunder boomed over their heads. Carrie jumped. She glanced out her window praying to not see it again. She didn't.

"An animal?... Yes," she said catching her breath. "But, it wasn't dead. It was... digging, I think."

"Digging?" Steve asked.

Carrie nodded. "And it was... *big*... like a bigfoot, or a werewolf, or *something*."

They spent the next few minutes in silence. The news on the radio gave way to Garth Brooks' The Thunder Rolls. Carrie glanced at Steve, who had his eyes glued to the highway, wondering what he was thinking.

I know what he's thinking. He's thinking this is just like all the other times.

And he'd be right. It was just like the other times. All the times when she had seen something no one else had seen. She knew he didn't believe her, but she also knew, deep down, Steve wanted to believe.

This had been happening to Carrie her entire life. It began with seeing odd creatures outside her bedroom window when she was nine, by twelve the ghostly lights in the sky appeared. It was as if they followed her everywhere, and only she saw them.

No, that's not right. Others would see them—those UFOs, aliens, guardian-damned-angels. Fuck if I know what they are—but it was like their brains had a filter blocking out the truth of what their eyes saw.

And these things would vanish every time she attempted to point them out to others. The creatures were even more elusive than the lights—because they got away faster, and came around less often—and for that, she was glad.

Thank God for small favors. Carrie thought. *Those nasty things scare the shit out of me.*

She looked out the window, remembering the thing she had seen a few moments ago.

Was it one of them? Surely not all the way out here, and none of them had been that *big* before. *Maybe I had seen a bigfoot after all?*

Carrie found some strange comfort in that thought and then shuddered. *Carrie, you are one seriously fucked up chick, you know that?* Yes, unfortunately, she knew that all too well.

The rain was harder now, falling in thick crystalline sheets. She stared through the water as it twisted and distorted the roadway ahead of them. She admired the hypnotic symphony of white lines and reflected halogen glow until something out ahead of them grabbed her attention.

"Steve, do you see that?"

Steve gave a reluctant sigh and looked out toward her side of the highway. He expected to see nothing, but was surprised by the bright orange object they were approaching. Through the blurry, rain streaked windshield, he recognized the diamond shaped road sign but couldn't make out what it said.

"Did you catch that?" he asked glancing to his wife.

"Road Construction... Flagger Ahead."

"I heard nothing on the traffic reports about construction," Steve said perplexed. He turned the radio dial and Garth hissed out of existence, replaced by silence.

He kept turning until the numbers looped back to the beginning and stopped at the station that had been playing The Thunder Rolls, now just as silent as the others. Steve turned the volume up. A steady hiss of static poured from the speakers. It was as if the entire world had vanished from the airwaves. Steve shut the radio off.

"I know we aren't that far into the hills, must be the weather."

Carrie didn't say a word. She looked pale. He began to ask her a question then stopped. He had seen that look before—the answers to questions that followed that look were never pleasant.

Steve lost himself in memories of the last time he saw that look on Carrie's face. They had stopped at a rest area a few hours before the storm began. Steve checked the Toyota's oil while Carrie used the restroom. Steve walked up to wash his hands when she came out holding the tiny white stick in her hand. The look on her face told him the answer. They had been trying to get pregnant for months.

Carrie turned to face the wall, not wanting him to see the tears welling up in her eyes. Steve, not wanting to leave her alone just now, opted to use the drinking fountain to clean his hands and dried them on his jeans. He hugged his arms around her and said nothing. He knew she responded to his touch more than words.

They were both staring at the bulletin board next to the state highway map that was telling them *YOU ARE HERE*. The board was almost filled with missing person flyers. Steve had never seen so many in one place. He looked at the faces of men, women, and *children*. His mind went to the child he may never have, then Carrie began to hum.

That haunting tune of hers she always hummed or sang. The tune he remembers from the first time they met; when the whole world except for *her* vanished. Nothing he could do but go to *her*.

He forgot about the child that wasn't. The world slipped away, and all that remained was Carrie and her song.

Carrie shaking his arm brought him back to the present. "Steve look," her voice trembled.

Up ahead of them orange and white construction barrels, spaced across the two-lane highway, blocked the road. A sign—illuminated by road flares —read *DETOUR* and the arrow pointed to a tiny dirt road that cut into the forest to the right of the highway. Orange cones placed on the roadway carved a curved path onto it.

Behind the barricade of barrels stood a tall man wearing a high visibility vest and a hard hat — his resemblance to a road-worker ended there. He waved a large lava-lamp shaped flashlight toward the dirt road.

Steve slowed down as they approached this scene, watching the man. His face invisible in the dark except for every few seconds when his waving flashlight passed by. Steve was trying to piece together the flashes of the man's image to get an idea of what he looked like. He could make out a rather large, unnaturally elongated, chin. Deep coarse wrinkles—*or were they scars?*—marked his face. And deep-set red eyes. *Red? No, that must have been the reflection of the road flares playing tricks of light... right?*

"I don't see any construction," Carrie said peering through the windshield, "and why would anyone work in this weather anyhow?" She looked at the dirt road the sign and that odd worker were directing them to. "Steve, I don't want to go down *there.*"

"Neither do I, but we have little choice," Steve pulled off the highway and onto the detour. There was brief rumble of gravel under the tires as the pavement transitioned into dirt. Steve let out his breath, which he hadn't realized he'd been holding in since he looked at that strange man.

The little Toyota's shocks yelled out in agony as it rocked up and down over the unpaved road. Crooked branches scratched across the sides of the vehicle. The headlights did little to light their way through the pitchy blackness.

Steve looked in the rear-view mirror and could no longer see the lights from the highway. He glanced down at the fuel gauge—less than a quarter tank—and hoped that this detour wasn't a long one.

———

"Steve, slow down!" Carrie hollered noticing how fast the car had propelled itself through the forest-walled tunnel the road had become. The only things visible outside: trees, and dark.

"We don't have a lot of gas honey... I don't want to get stuck *out here*."

Carrie looked at Steve's face, unnerved by what she saw there. She had always known her husband to be strong and fearless. What she saw now, growing in his features was uncertainty and fear.

A large shadowy thing bounded into their path. Steve slammed the brakes. There was a brief crunch of metal, then the shrill scraping of claws against steel and glass as the huge creature rolled onto the hood and scurried up the windshield onto the roof. Silence. Long scratches scarred the windshield.

They looked at each other with the same thought—*What the hell was that?* Steve hit the gas and the car jumped forward; the thing rolled down the back windshield, across the trunk, and onto the ground with a wet thud.

They both turned peering out the back. "Go, just go!" Carrie yelled, but Steve just sat there; eyes wide, jaw dropped.

"I want to find out what the hell that was."

"It's just a stupid bear. This is the forest Steve."

He looked at her with gaped amazement, "we both saw that thing... *that* wasn't a bear."

"Whatever it is, it's dangerous... look what it did to the windshield!"

"I think I killed it. Is that what you saw earlier on the side of the highway?"

A low rumbling growl from behind the car answered Steve's question. A monstrous clawed paw —covered in coarse dark gray fur—reached up and gripped the trunk.

"*Shit!*" Steve shifted into drive and floored the gas pedal. The car launched into motion and the paw fell away; the claws ripping jagged lines through the metal. Steve looked in the mirror: it stood up on two legs and roared, its eyes— reflecting the taillights—glowed red in the rain.

As far as Carrie could tell the creature did not follow them. Keeping herself turned to the back seat, she watched for it to come charging up the road. She was unprepared for the sudden stop when Steve slammed on the brakes once again. Carrie flew toward the dash and would have cracked her skull had she not been gripping the car seat so tightly out of fear. Pulling herself back up, she saw Steve panting for breath. She followed his eyes to see the old rusted junker that sat across the one lane road. There was no way past it: the forest's edge encroached upon both sides.

"What kind of fucking detour is this?" Steve exclaimed.

Steve killed the engine and listened, expecting to hear the wet patter of huge paws rushing toward them. No sounds came out of the forest.

"What do we do now?" Carrie asked, holding back tears, but Steve could hear them in her voice. He opened his door and stood up without exiting, raising his head up over the roof to get a better look ahead of them, past the junked car.

"I think I see a light up there," Steve said as he reached in and turned off the headlights, "looks like a porch-light... let's go."

"Go?" Carrie asked surprised, "go where?"

"Well, we can't just sit *here*, maybe we can use their phone? Our other choice is to go back toward that *thing*," Steve grabbed a flashlight from the backseat, shut the door, and walked around the junker. Having no choice, Carrie got out and followed him.

The cabin wasn't hard to find, the dirt road led

right to it, and then ended. Steve saw a sign post sticking up from the ground. He raised his flash-light beam up the rusted skeletal remains of the post until it came to rest upon the sign perched at the top. **NO OUTLET**.

"Great fucking detour!" Steve spat out. He looked at Carrie, who was staring off to the far right of the cabin.

"Look over there," Carrie said and Steve swung the beam over in the direction she was pointing. The light revealed dozens of old, stripped-down, rusted out cars scattered all about the clearing surrounding the cabin.

"I think I hear an engine; maybe the road continues over there?" Steve took his wife's hand into his and they walked.

"There's your engine," Carrie stopped next to an odd generator homemade from a car engine. "This means they don't have city power, and likely they won't have a phone either," Steve said as he climbed up the porch steps. Carrie, right behind him, followed.

The porch-light that had led them to the cabin was an industrial size bug zapper; like the generator, it was also homemade. A wooden frame covered with chicken wire; electrical wires led to a rusty fuse box. Below the bug zapper was a rotting pile of flies, mosquitoes, and various other unidentified insects.

The windows, boarded up from the inside, left no way to tell if there were lights on. Steve knocked and listened for footsteps. After a few seconds, he knocked again and put his ear to the door.

"Steve..."

"Shh, I hear something in there."

"Steve..."

"Carrie, I'm try—"

She grabbed his shoulder and spun him around. He looked back toward where they left the car and saw the huge, shadowy bulk, and the glowing eyes. *"Shit!"* He wheeled around and pounded on the cabin door. The door opened.

"Come in, *hurry*," whispered a soft female voice.

Steve grabbed Carrie's hand and pulled her inside. A young woman shut the door behind them.

The inside of the cabin, bathed in shadow, was lit by a few candles. The woman stood in darkness by the door. "You'll be safe in here," her voice was almost a perpetual whisper.

"What's out there?" Steve asked between heavy gulps of breath.

"The Night... It has teeth," She moved away from the door, her movements were fluid, she seemed to almost glide. Steve still could not make out her face in the candle light. Carrie had her face pressed into Steve's shoulder sobbing from fear. He rubbed her back and made shushing sounds.

"Does this road have an outlet... Miss?" Steve asked as the woman entered what appeared to be the kitchen.

"Road?" she laughed, the sound almost a giggle. "That is our driveway, there are no roads here."

"Then why the hell did the construction detour us through here?"

"I do not know... that is most odd," her voice came from farther away; she was no longer in sight.

Steve sat Carrie onto a couch, the plastic covering crinkled beneath her. He kissed her then turned to walk into the room the woman had gone into. "Listen, do you have a telephone or something?"

"Miss?" Steve said as he entered the empty kitchen, lit by a three-candle sconce sitting on the table. She was nowhere to be found.

"Weird...," Steve turned to go back to Carrie and ran straight into the wall. The doorway he walked through was gone. *"Owe! What the fuck?"*

He spun around in a complete circle. Nothing, but four walls.

"Steve," a sultry young female voice echoed to him from behind.

He turned to see the woman ascending a staircase that was now where a wall stood a moment before. He saw her shapely legs under the sheer nightgown, and then she vanished up the stairs.

This is nuts, he told himself. *I'm losing it.*

"Hey, stop!" Steve shouted and stepped to the bottom of the stairs.

She was gone. He stared up into the dark and then he heard the song. The sweet lulling tune he knew so well. Carrie's song. Without knowing what he was doing, he climbed the stairs.

———

Carrie sat motionless on the couch, unblinking, her lips moving; mouthing words, but no sound escaped them. She kept repeating what that woman had said, over and over in her mind. *The Night... it has teeth—The Night... it has teeth—The Night...* She was startled out of her shock by the sound of the front door knob turning.

"Steve—," she yelled out for him, but then fell silent when she saw the solid wall where he had gone. The door opened and a man walked in closing the door behind him. He was very tall and lanky from what she could see in the room, now lit by one candle, which sat on the mantel.

He stepped toward her and she saw the orange vest he was wearing. *It's that road-worker, what's he doing...?* Her thought cut off as he stepped close enough for her to see his face, covered with deep-set wrinkles. He must have been a hundred years old. Closer. No, not wrinkles. Scars, severely *deep* scars—his face ruined with them. Closer. No, not scars...

They were now bleeding, dripping wounds—a piece of flesh fell from his face and smacked wetly onto the floor. Carrie screamed.

"I'm sorry, did I scare you," his voice was deep and rough, almost a growl, "maybe you'll like this better?" In a blink of her eye, his face appeared healed and young. Even his filthy construction clothes had now become a new clean suit.

"We've been calling you home baby," he said, his voice now sweet and gentle. He took her hands and lifted her from the couch. "Come now, your sisters are waiting to see you," he said then whistled a tune. *Her* tune. *How does he know my song?* She wanted to resist, but all she could do was follow.

Steve followed the song up the stairs. The door at the top opened for him and he entered without pausing. Inside his mind, he was yelling at himself to stop, but the song was too strong.

That siren song filled his skull with sweet hypnotic tones. The room inside was lit with a single bulb hanging from the ceiling. It flickered on and off, creating a disorienting strobe effect. In front of him was the woman lying on a bed. He could see her during the brief flickers of the bulb. She writhed on the bed, the sheets—some kind of clear vinyl or plastic—made low crinkling sounds beneath her. The song continued, in-between heavy panting breaths. He could see she was rubbing herself. She was getting herself off. He was drawn to her.

As he approached the bed, another woman appeared to his right. He looked at her. Carrie? No, it wasn't her. The eyes were not Carrie's eyes, but her face was nearly identical. Her mouth opened and she joined the singing of the song. Steve stood frozen, his mind torn between the two sirens he could not resist; and the desperate internal need to *RUN*.

His mind reaches out desperately for a piece of familiar reality and finds a memory to cling to.

———

Night. Autumn. Rosewood Park. Steve is walking home from the bookstore after work. He's taking a shortcut through the park which really isn't shorter, but he doesn't care because it's a lovely night and he wants to enjoy it. As he passes the swings in the playground, he hears humming. He can't help going toward it. She's beautiful; the young woman, humming as she swings herself back and forth. He goes to her, and after that moment, never spends another day apart from her.

This is where Steve meets Carrie. Where Steve hears the siren song for the first time. This will be the last song Steve ever hears.

———

"You always were such an independent child," the man was leading her up the stairs talking in a sweet tone as he went. Up ahead of them, she could hear the singing and insane laughter of women and the anguished screams of a man. She recognized the screams as Steve's. She wanted to run away, run for help, run until daylight, but her body held fast and kept walking. The man continued talking.

"I had told you so many times not to go out in the day, but no, you refused to listen to your father, like a good little siren. You sneaked out to play in the light, you wandered too close to the road, and they found you. Those awful people took you away. Mistook you for one of them. Raised you as their own. We called for you. We sent the creatures of the night to find you and bring you back home. But, you didn't understand our lullaby anymore, although you still sang it, and the creatures frightened you. You had forgotten us. *They* made you forget. Made you think that your memories were only childhood nightmares. But we found a way to bring you home."

They reached the top; he pushed the door open and then shoved her inside.

"Now go say hello to your sisters, they're waiting for you," he snarled.

She stumbled and fell to her knees at the foot of the bed. The two women were kneeling side by side on top of it, their heads down. Carrie could see in the flickering of the light that their nightgowns were bloody. They raised and turned toward her in unison.

Blood and gore dripped from fanged snouts and she could recognize herself in them despite their transformation. Steve's ruined body lay between them. A river of red flowed down the plastic sheets and pooled on the floor where Carrie knelt.

The man who had called himself her father cackled like a devil behind her. She turned and saw the beast from the forest. His fur covered snout spread in a hideous grin, saliva dripped from razor teeth.

Carrie sobbed into her hands, now covered in Steve's blood and bits of flesh. The blood mingled with her tears creating a red saline slush that coated her face. The salty smell filled her senses. It was the smell of the ocean. It was the smell of ghost ships, sea monsters, and watery graves.

Carrie licked her hands and smiled.

It was the smell of ***home***.

AFTERWORD

Thank you for taking the time to read my story. I hope that you enjoyed reading it as much as I enjoyed writing it. I have only one request; if you did like it, please leave a review. Reviews are the lifeblood of indie and small press authors and greatly help us get more books in front of more readers. If you didn't like it, that's fine too, just leave an honest review, that's all I ask.

ABOUT THE AUTHOR

Randy Speeg is a horror, supernatural, and science-fiction writer from Cincinnati, Ohio. When he's not writing he is an active Libertarian, and also a Union President at his day job. He has been known to moonlight, on occasion, as a paranormal investigator. Randy is currently working on his first novel.

www.RandySpeegAuthor.com

ALSO BY RANDY SPEEG

The Fears and Dreams of Everlasting Life